OLD SAM
Jasper
AND MR FRANK

o

OLD SAM
Jasper
AND MR FRANK

o

TREVOR TODD

o

Illustrated by Betty Greenhatch

Published with the assistance of the
Literature Board of the Australia Council

Viking Kestrel

Viking Kestrel
Penguin Books Australia Ltd,
487 Maroondah Highway, P.O. Box 257
Ringwood, Victoria, 3134, Australia
Penguin Books Ltd,
Harmondsworth, Middlesex, England
Penguin Books,
40 West 23rd Street, New York, N.Y. 10010, U.S.A.
Penguin Books Canada Ltd,
2801 John Street, Markham, Ontario, Canada
Penguin Books (N.Z.) Ltd,
182-190 Wairau Road, Auckland 10, New Zealand

First published 1985 by Viking

Typeset in Century Old Style by Dudley E. King, Melbourne
Made and printed in Australia by
The Dominion Press-Hedges & Bell, Victoria

CIP

Todd, Trevor, 1947–
Old Sam, Jasper and Mr Frank.

ISBN 0 670 80692 7.

1. Children's stories, Australian. I. Greenhatch,
Betty, 1941–   . II. Title.

A823'.3

For Annaliese

O·N·E

Old Sam Lindsay had been retired more years than anyone could remember. He had lived in the same weatherboard weather-beaten house with his wife, Beryl, since they were first married. Their inner-city suburb had changed a great deal since they had lived there. But Old Sam hadn't changed.

Sam's one great interest in life was his chickens. He had six of them and each one had a name. He spent hours each day watching them and Old Sam would swear that they understood when he talked to them. If ever Old Sam had an argument with Beryl he would stomp off to the backyard with mutterings like, 'At least my chickens don't nag me!'

Each afternoon Old Sam would lean on his wrought-iron front gate to watch the rush-hour crowds escaping from the city. Not many cars came down Albert Road. It was narrow and led only to the football ground. Occasionally Sam would get a wave or an 'Evening' from one of the passers-by but most of the noise came from the choked highway at the top end of the road.

The paper-boy wasn't sure what to make of Old Sam. Some days as he pedalled up to the house he would get a smile or a 'Hello, young feller.' Other days Old Sam would hardly speak or growl that his paper was late – even when it wasn't.

Old Sam didn't like kids. Sam and Beryl Lindsay didn't have any children of their own. The older boys in the district thought that Old Sam was strange and that he was fun to tease. Especially the Kemp twins. They were the worst. They were identical twins – turned-up noses, pug-faces and short bristly hair – it was almost impossible to tell them apart. They seemed always to be laughing. Not a happy, friendly laugh, but a laugh which found pleasure in hurting other people.

One day, as the Kemp twins turned into Albert Road kicking their football and jostling each other into the gutter, they caught sight of Old Sam leaning on his gate. Whispering together, they crossed the street so that they would walk right past Old Sam.

'Hey, Chickabiddy, is Esmeralda's wing better?' jeered Gary in a voice of mock concern. 'Chickabiddy' was the nickname the older boys had given him. He didn't like it. Old Sam furrowed his brow and looked the other way. Peter tried to stifle his laughter.

'Puck, puck, puck ...' clucked Gary with his arms folded back like wings. He strutted up and down in front of the old man, waving his arms, pretending to be a chicken. Old Sam tried to ignore him.

'Puck, puck ... Is Myrtle laying?' Grunts of stifled laughter broke from Peter. 'Puck, puck!' Gary was enjoying himself. 'Puck, puck ... PARK! Hey Chickabiddy!' He was half squatting and flapping his arms. 'I just laid an egg!' The other boy snorted with laughter.

Old Sam jutted out his chin.

'Blasted kids,' he thought. 'If I was a few years younger ...' He turned and moved off towards his front door. The crack of the rock hitting the iron roof stopped him. It sounded like a pistol-shot. The stone rolled noisily down the corrugated iron and dropped into the guttering. Old Sam turned as a second and a third stone hit the roof.

'Hey!' But the Kemp twins had raced off towards the

football ground. 'You ... Blasted kids!' His face was red and his chest rose and fell. 'Miserable kids! You wait till I ...'

As they disappeared round the corner, the boys' insane laughter echoed back to mock the helpless old man. 'Chick, chick. Here, Chicky!'

'I'm calling the police!' Old Sam shouted after them. 'I'll go and see your father. That's what I'll do!' His voice was hoarse and breathless. He glared down the empty street.

Beryl appeared at the front door.

'Sam? Sam? What is it?'

'Kids!' exploded Sam, even angrier because his threats had been so useless. 'Those blasted Kemp twins. Throwing stones on our roof. Brats!' Old Sam brushed past and stomped into the house. 'Kids! Kids these days! In my day you could expect a good hiding if you gave cheek to your elders like that. Throwing stones on our roof! Where's the phone book? I'll call the police. That's what I'm going to do, Beryl!'

'Sam ... I don't know.' Beryl straightened her apron. 'They've gone now. Let's ... let's just leave it be.'

'Leave it be?' shouted Sam. 'Leave it be? Vandals! Young vandals! – Just forget it? They deserve horse-whipping, that pair of hooligans. That's what they deserve!'

'If you involve the police, Sam ... It's just not worth it.'

'Pah, if I catch them!'

'Sam, don't get yourself in a state, now. Remember

what Doctor Jacob said.'

Sam banged the telephone book down on the sideboard.

'Let 'em get away with it?' His big frame sagged. 'If I was a few years younger, Beryl...'

'Yes, Sam.'

Old Sam moved to the front door, then back again. 'I'm going up to feed me chickens.' The old man ambled out the back door. Beryl gazed after him.

T·W·O

Over the next few days Old Sam spent less time leaning on his front gate and even more time with his chickens. He had built the cage himself years before when he was more active. The weatherboards had long ago faded and cracked but the cage was still strong.

Old Sam also spent more time in his shed. It too had seen better days. The unpainted wooden boards had turned grey with so many seasons of sun and rain. But it was dry inside. The shed was a junk merchant's paradise. Old chests and a wardrobe stood piled high with boxes. Although it looked a jumble Old Sam knew where everything was. A scratched metal cigar box contained medals earned by Old Sam's father in a long-ago war. A cardboard box contained a vacuum cleaner which didn't work, and in another box Sam kept a car radio and speakers, even though he had never owned a car. In front of the dusty, cobwebbed window was Sam's work-bench. He still kept his carpentry tools although he didn't use them much these days.

Old Sam was in his shed when he heard noises coming

from the next house. He peered through the dusty window, but couldn't see anything, so decided to take a stroll to the front to see what was happening. Albert Road was usually quiet. Old Sam got quite a shock as he approached his front gate.

A huge removal truck blocked the street. It had stopped outside the house next to Old Sam's. Three men dressed in blue overalls were struggling to lower the enormous door at the rear. The truck was longer than the house. Old Sam couldn't remember when the house next door had last been lived in. The backyard was a mass of tangled weeds. It looked as though Old Sam and Beryl were to have new neighbours.

A battered car drew up behind the truck. Old Sam

couldn't contain his surprise. ''Struth!' He ambled up to his front door and went inside.

'Beryl. Beryl?'

'What's up, Sam?' asked Beryl as she wiped her hands on a tea-towel.

'Take a look at this!' Old Sam went into the front room and stood by the curtain. Beryl followed.

'We're going to have neighbours again!' she exclaimed. 'That'll be nice.'

'Take another look,' said Sam, peering past the curtain. A woman and three children had got out of the battered car and were talking to the men at the rear of the truck.

'Aboriginals,' huffed Sam.

'Well?' demanded Beryl.

'You know . . .' said the old man awkwardly.

'They've got a right to live there, Sam. What a size that truck is!'

'Don't you see, Beryl, with Aboriginals living next door . . .'

'They've got to live somewhere,' interrupted Beryl.

Old Sam became annoyed. He tramped off to the kitchen. Beryl stayed for a moment watching furniture emerging from the back of the truck, then went back to her kitchen. Old Sam was pacing up and down by the kitchen table.

'You mark my words, Beryl. With Aboriginals living next door . . . the value of this property will go down. You mark my words!'

'Property value?' exclaimed Beryl with a laugh. 'You'll never want to sell this house of ours, Sam. And you know it. Where would we move to? So what does property value mean to us?'

9

Old Sam didn't reply but stuck out his chin and rubbed the back of his neck against his collar.

'Kids!' he said suddenly. 'Three kids – *boys*, too! They'll be kicking their footballs over the fence and climbing into our back garden. You mark my words.'

Beryl gave another laugh of surprise. 'So that's what's worrying you. Those kids looked all right to me. I think I'll pop next door when they've settled and say hello.'

'What!' snapped Old Sam clenching and unclenching his fists. 'And you can tell them that if I catch them in our backyard – watch out!'

'Sam!'

'I'm going up to see me chickens!' He shuffled out the back door.

And so Sam and Beryl Lindsay had neighbours. Like any change in Albert Road, Old Sam didn't like it but he put up with it. He was never bad mannered or anything like that. But he wasn't friendly, either.

T·H·R·E·E

Old Sam's routine was to be upset sooner than he thought. He didn't usually spill any wheat as he fetched it from the shed, and he always closed the creaking wooden door after him. On this day he didn't. Old Sam ambled off to feed his chickens.

There was a beating of wings, an arc of white underwing. It stopped. A bird had landed on the path outside the shed door. It stood and looked nervously from side to side. It was poised, ready to take off again in an instant.

Near the railway yard dozens of pigeons could be found. They were marked by grease smears and had scraggly feathers and lean bodies. This one was different. His eyes were clear. His body was sleek, not gaunt, and the feathers looked as if they had been tuned for racing. It must have been a racer because there was a metal band around the right leg.

Satisfied that it was in no immediate danger the pigeon pecked hungrily at the wheat on the path. Every now and then it flicked its wings as if it was ready to take off, in a hurry if necessary. The grains of wheat led the hungry bird up to the open door. The bird hesitated, cocking its head for danger, but hunger won and it pecked its way into Sam's shed.

Old Sam came shuffling back along the path carrying a tin tray of eggs. He noticed the open door and moved to close it. There was a flurry of flapping and white underwing. In his haste to shut the door Old Sam almost dropped the eggs. He put the tray carefully on the path, then opened the shed door a fraction and peered in.

''Struth!' exclaimed Sam. 'A pigeon – and a fat one, too!' The pigeon was pressed hard against the dusty shed window. It clung to the wooden sill. The outstretched wings raised clouds of dust. Sam closed the door again, picked up the tray, then hurried to the kitchen.

'Beryl!' puffed Old Sam as he put the eggs on the kitchen table. 'A pigeon. I've gone and caught myself a pigeon in the shed. Pretty little feller. A fat one, too. How long since we had pigeon pie, Beryl? How long is it?'

The surprised Beryl thought for a moment.

'Donkey's years!' she laughed.

'That's right – donkey's years. Heh! Get the pie-dish out, Beryl. And make some pastry. We're going to have pigeon pie for tea tonight.'

With a spring in his step and whistling a tuneless song Old Sam walked up the path. Pigeon pie! Behind Sam's shed was the woodpile. He walked past the stacked wood to the chopping-block, pulled out his axe and headed for the shed. At the door he stopped and rubbed at his stubbly chin with the back of his hand. He'd have to be careful, otherwise the bird would escape and he wouldn't get his pie for tea. Old Sam leaned his axe against the wall

12

and in a surprisingly agile movement opened the door, slipped inside, then closed it behind him.

The bird was still pressed against the window. It nodded its head uncertainly as if it sensed what was in Sam's mind. The old man stared at the bird. It seemed a pity, he thought. Such a beautiful bird. Surely a thoroughbred. Flecked silver feathers lined the throat.

Over the fine body the steel-grey feathers were speckled with chocolate-brown. The long wing and tail feathers

were the colour of gun-metal. Still Old Sam stared, unable to move. The red-pink feet clawed at the wooden sill. The clear eyes darted alertly. Each feather fitted in perfect shape. Such a pity.

Sam edged forward, arms raised, fingers outstretched. A frantic flapping of wings stirred balloons of dust. Jars of nails and a tin can were knocked sideways. Old Sam crouched out of sight and, squinting, waited for the right moment.

On the other side of the window in the new neighbours' backyard a young, brown face stared wide-eyed, first at the trapped bird, then at the two hands which appeared behind the glass. They hesitated for a second, then closed on the bird. For a moment it appeared to be squashed against the window as fingers groped for a tighter grip, then hands and bird disappeared from view.

With the bird in one hand and the axe in the other Old Sam headed for the chopping-block. Stooping, he regarded the bird for what he thought would be the last time. With a final shrug Old Sam lifted the axe high.

'Are you going to kill that bird?'

'What!' Old Sam swung around, surprised, guilty. A small Aboriginal boy stared at him through a gap in the picket fence.

'What the . . .! Kids! Clear off!'

The brown eyes still stared at him.

'Are you going to kill that bird, Mr Chickabiddy?'

'What!' Old Sam couldn't bring himself to prepare the pigeon pie with those eyes staring at him from the gap in the fence. He let the axe drop to the ground.

'Are you the kid who's been sneaking into my backyard? I've seen the footprints. I'll skin any kid I catch coming into my backyard. Is that clear?'

'I've never been in your backyard, Mr Chickabiddy.'

Sam grew angry and his chin jutted out.

'Cheeky kids! Who told you to call me that?'

'I heard some of the kids in the street call you Mr Chickabiddy. Why are you going to kill it? It's a real pretty bird, Mister.'

Old Sam felt his nerve drain away. The brown eyes stared unblinkingly at him.

Sam rubbed the back of his neck against his collar and coughed. 'The name's Lindsay. Sam Lindsay. Everybody in this district knows me. Don't you go listening to those boys in the street.'

The old man stood up and looked at the bird. It seemed so frail enclosed in his huge, time-worn hand. Its legs and wings were trapped. Only the head moved with freedom.

'Course I'm not going to kill the blasted bird.' Old Sam coughed. 'And you mind what I said about not coming into this back garden!' He moved off to the shed. The axe was left at the woodpile.

Old Sam left the pigeon locked in his shed and went off to tell Beryl about the change in the dinner arrangements.

F·O·U·R

Old Sam found Beryl kneeling on the kitchen floor surrounded by pots and baking trays. She was reaching into the back of a cupboard.

'Is that you, Sam? I've got that tray I use to make for my steak-and-kidney pies. It's only a small bird, isn't it?'

'Er... Beryl.' Old Sam scratched his head. 'Beryl, I got to thinking. We don't know where it's been. You know, it might have disease or lice or something. Perhaps it's best if we don't kill it – er, eat it.'

Beryl stood up.

'Oh. All right, Sam. I thought you said it was a clean one. "Pretty little feller" you said.'

'Yes, but... better be on the safe side.'

'Have you let it go?'

'No, it's, er, in my shed,' answered Old Sam.

'I thought I saw you walking up to the woodpile with something under your arm?' questioned Beryl, suspiciously.

'Yes, but I, er... It's back in the shed now. I thought perhaps we could let it go, or, seeing how it's such a pretty little feller we could give it to one of Dawn's kids,' said Old Sam awkwardly.

'Dawn's kids? We see them about twice a year, Sam. The inside of your shed would be a right old mess by the time Dawn drops in to see us again,' laughed Beryl. 'I know what. You could give it to one of those boys next door.'

'What? Why them? That crowd wouldn't know what to do with it!' huffed Old Sam.

'Go on. Didn't cost you anything. They haven't got any pets.' Old Sam jutted out his chin then trudged out the back door mumbling as he went. 'And mind it doesn't escape when you're trying to catch it,' Beryl shouted after him. 'You caught it before, all right!' Old Sam didn't reply.

He caught the pigeon more easily a second time and walked up to the picket fence behind the shed. The boy wasn't there. Old Sam peered over the fence and went to call out, but suddenly realized he didn't know the boy's name.

'Boy. Boy?' called Old Sam feeling silly. 'Are you there, boy?'

The back door banged and the small boy emerged staring wide-eyed at the old man calling him from the other side of the fence.

Sam looked awkward. 'Look, I've just had an idea. Come into my garden and I'll tell you.' The boy eyed the old man suspiciously and didn't speak. 'I know I just told you not to come into my garden but ... I've got something for you. Come round by the front gate. Mind you close it after you, though.'

The boy disappeared. A few moments later he came

shyly towards Old Sam, then stopped some distance away. Now that they were face to face without a fence between them the boy avoided Sam's eyes and looked shyly at his feet. He was barefoot and his grey shorts seemed two sizes too large. His arms and legs were slender, angular, and he wore a school jumper without a shirt underneath. Sam didn't recognize the school colours.

'What's your name, son?' asked Sam.

'Jasper,' replied the boy. He was staring at the pigeon in the old man's hand.

'Jasper!' snorted Sam. 'What sort of a name is that? Used to have a dog named Jasper!'

'It's my name,' said the boy.

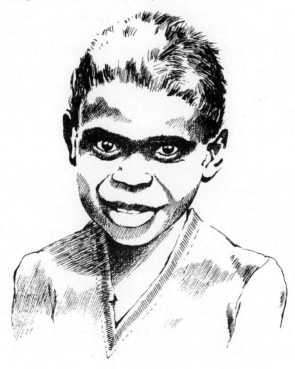

'Er, yeah, son.' Old Sam rubbed the back of his neck against his collar. He looked down at the bird in his hand. 'It's like this, son.' Sam gave a deep sigh. I've got no use for a pigeon. I've got my chickens to look after. Look – you have the pigeon. Didn't cost me anything, anyway.'

Sam held the bird out to the boy. Jasper looked down and shuffled his feet.

'Well,' huffed Sam. 'No need to get excited about it, I must say. In my day if a bloke gave you something you put a smile on your face and said, "Thank you".'

Jasper, head down, turned to go.

'Wait . . . ' Old Sam was puzzled.

Still the boy stared down at his feet. Sam was embarrassed by the silence. He coughed. After what seemed a minute the boy spoke softly.

'I got nowhere to keep it. And my older brothers. They would let it out. I know they would. I had a canary once. They let it go.'

Old Sam looked at the pigeon in his hand and then at the boy.

'Er . . . tell you what, son, we'll put him in with my chickens until we work out what to do with it. Just temporary. He's yours, though. No cats can get at him. Safe as houses. He'll need a perch. He'd be bossed around by my chickens if he had to share a perch with them.'

Jasper smiled.

'That's more like it, son. Serious little feller, aren't you. When I was a boy we'd be fishing and laughing . . . ' His voice trailed off. 'Here. You take him for a minute while I find a bit of wood and a hammer and some nails. Careful now.'

The boy took the bird into his hands gingerly, reverently, not wanting to crush it but not wanting to let it escape. The bird was frightened. Jasper was surprised to feel the heart beating. The outer feathers felt cool and slippery but the under-feathers were warm and soft. He held the bird level with his face and regarded it as if it was the world champion pigeon.

From the door of his shed Old Sam watched the boy.

'What are you going to call it?' asked Sam.

The boy looked surprised.

'Yes, . . . you. He's your bird, isn't he? So you've got to give it a name, see?'

Jasper gave a wide, embarrassed grin, looked at the bird and then at Old Sam.

'Mr Frank!' announced Jasper.

'Mr Frank?' spluttered Old Sam. 'Mr Frank? Funny name for a bird. Kids these days! Still, Mr Frank it is then. Bring him over here. Time to introduce *Mr Frank* to the other residents. Heh!'

21

The boy released the bird into the chickens' cage and it flew to the far end. With wings outstretched and red feet clawing to the wire it hung there, looking up at the sky. The chickens took no notice of the pigeon but looked hopefully towards Old Sam as if expecting some extra scraps.

Jasper watched as Old Sam expertly nailed the new perch into position in a high corner of the wooden cage.

'There. Right as rain. Now,' puffed Old Sam as he closed the cage door behind him and rolled down his sleeves, 'I'll be darned if I'm going to feed and water your bird all the time. He'll most likely get some of the chickens' wheat but it's your job to come round here every day and make sure he's getting his fair share. Understand? Take some of the chickens' wheat from the shed, if you like. And poke the hose through the wire just here and make sure the water-trough is cleaned out each day. You come round here tomorrow and I'll show you where everything's kept. You go to school, don't you?' The boy nodded. 'And make sure you close the door after you. If my chickens get into Mrs Lindsay's vegetable patch there'll be hell to pay. So you remember that.'

'Thanks . . . Mr Sam.'

'Off you go, now, boy. I'll see you here tomorrow.'

The boy left and Old Sam turned and ambled towards the kitchen. He sat down at the kitchen table and spread out the evening newspaper.

'I heard some banging coming from the chickens' cage,' remarked Beryl as she dropped slices of bacon into the frypan.

'Yes,' said Old Sam not taking his eyes from the

newspaper. 'I gave the pigeon to the little fellow next
door and he pleaded with me to let him keep it in with the

chickens.' Sam turned a page. 'Just temporary, like, until he organizes a cage.'

Beryl smiled.

'That's nice, Sam,' she said.

F·I·V·E

'I was just passing the grain-feed store and I thought I might as well get this. Here. But don't think that I can afford to do this every week,' said Old Sam.

Jasper took the paper bag from Old Sam and picked at the top. Inside was a cellophane packet full of dry brown peas.

'Pigeon peas. Gives them a change in their diet. You watch Mr Frank go for them.'

Old Sam had his hammer and nails and pieces of wood outside the chickens' cage. He had been waiting for school to finish so that Jasper could help.

'It's like this, see. If we build a little platform high up inside the cage, then the bird can have his feed up there away from the chickens. And this wooden box...If we nail it next to the platform, he'll be able to hop in there and keep out of the wind. What do you say, boy?'

Jasper grinned. 'That's good.'

'Now, you close the door after me so that your Mr Frank doesn't escape. Hand me the hammer.'

Jasper watched Old Sam puffing and hammering the

25

pieces of wood into place. When at last the platform was finished Old Sam called to Jasper.

'There's one way to make sure Mr Frank gets used to his new home – and quickly. Hand me the pigeon peas.' Sam placed some of the hard, dry peas up on the platform. The chickens eyed Sam eagerly. 'Pigeon peas are too expensive for the likes of you, Esmeralda,' chuckled Old Sam. 'Right. Let's see what Mr Frank thinks of the handiwork.'

Old Sam climbed out of the cage, then stepped back to watch the pigeon. The boy and the old man watched in silence. The bird flew from its position on the wire to the new platform. It greedily pecked at the peas until there were none left.

'He sure likes those pigeon peas, Mr Sam,' said Jasper. 'Shall I clean the water now?'

'Yes, son. You get in the cage and I'll hand you the hose. Then I'd better feed my chickens. They won't speak to me if they think I'm favouring your pigeon.'

Afterwards Old Sam showed Jasper the wheat-bin in his shed, then they sat down together on a rough wooden bench that Sam had built so he could watch his chickens.

'Greens,' said Old Sam. 'Your bird's got to get his greens. Lettuce scraps and bits like that. They like the odd bit of grit – stones and the like.'

'Stones?' asked Jasper. 'Why would he want stones?'

'Only little bits of grit. They store the wheat in their crop. See that bulge under those shiny feathers around the neck? That's the crop. They need the grit to help grind up the wheat. But clean water's the main thing. If you don't want your bird to get sick, keep his water clean. You mark my words.'

Jasper looked at Old Sam. 'Mr Sam, how come you know so much about keeping pigeons. Are they just like chickens?'

'No, son. No. My brother used to keep a few pigeons when he was a lad. That's going back a few years, I can tell you. But he's been dead . . . oh, donkey's years. Used to race them, too.'

'Race them?'

'Yes, but that's another story. First thing is to make sure Mr Frank likes his new home and keeps healthy. You mark my words, young feller. Better scoot home now. Your mother'll be wondering where you are.'

Jasper stood up. 'Bye, Mr Sam. And thanks.'

27

'That's all right, young feller. I'll see you tomorrow. Same time. Goodbye, now.'

Sam watched the boy go. He heard the clink of the front gate closing. From the other side of the picket fence Jasper's mother was calling. Old Sam shuffled towards the back door.

The weeks passed. Old Sam started to look forward to the boy's visits. Every day after school Jasper called in and the old man and the boy lingered over the needs of their very special pigeon. The 'temporary' arrangement of keeping Mr Frank in the chickens' cage was long forgotten.

Jasper was still a little unsure of Old Sam, though. On his good days the old man would settle back and tell Jasper about the old days: of living in the country, fishing; of home-cooked bread, trapping rabbits; and of lazy summers spent swimming in a warm, brown river. Other days Sam's wrinkled face seemed even more lined and he walked more stiffly, once or twice even using a walking-stick. On those days Old Sam would leave Jasper to feed his chickens. He wouldn't feel like talking and could only grumble about the weather or the state of the world.

As time went by Old Sam began to forget about the Kemp twins and the teasing and the stones on the roof. But the Kemp twins hadn't forgotten him.

On a warm evening when Old Sam and Beryl had settled themselves in front of the television to watch the news, two figures slipped noiselessly over the back fence and into Old Sam's yard. The moon was lost behind clouds. The two faces looked towards the pale glow of light coming from the side window and saw that the old couple were tucked away for the night. The boys looked at each other. Their faces were identical – turned-up noses, pug-faces and short bristly hair.

'They won't be coming out again tonight. Go on, do it.'

'Nah! You do it.'

'You're chicken!'

'You're chicken! You should be in that cage.'

'Cluck, cluck!'

Giggling, the two figures crept to the chickens' cage, opened the door and went in.

'Pooh! Smells in here!'

'No eggs. He must've collected 'em already.'

'Dopey chooks. You can walk right up to them in the dark.'

'Let's give 'em some flying lessons.'

'Yeah – exercise time.'

The sound of alarmed squawking filled the night.

Dazed chickens with outstretched wings crashed drunkenly into fence posts and shrubs. Feathers fluttered to the ground. A pigeon flapped awkwardly past the boys' faces, crashed sickeningly into the wire and dropped to the ground.

'Hey – he's got a pigeon in here. Chuck it out, too.'

The pigeon was thrown carelessly into the night sky. It flapped crazily and landed heavily on Old Sam's roof. The head bobbed uncertainly.

The two figures headed for the back fence. 'Smooth over your footprints. Here, where we landed coming over the fence. Come on. Last one over is a fried chook!'

More giggling, then the two figures disappeared over the back fence. The pale light still shone from the side window.

The next morning was not one of Sam's good days. He stayed in bed late and Jasper was at school by the time Old Sam went up to see his chickens.

S·I·X

'Beryl! Come and look! The chickens have got out! The pigeon's escaped, too!'

Beryl hurried as fast as her old legs would allow.

'Oh dear!' She put her hand to her mouth. 'Sam . . . I think one or two of them are hurt.'

The old man stood scowling by the empty cage. He turned.

''Struth! They've ruined your vegetable patch!' He marched over to the garden. A strand of white hair blew across his worried face. The lines in his forehead deepened. 'I think one's missing, Beryl. One, two . . .' He looked round the garden. 'Five! One's missing! And one's got a hurt wing!'

Sam strode back to the cage door. His chest was rising and falling and his fists were clenched.

'The door's open! That blasted boy must have left it open. He was the last one up here. To think I trusted him!'

'Are you sure, Sam?' asked Beryl becoming worried about her husband's growing temper. 'Could it have been

31

someone else?'

'Course I'm sure! No one else comes up here. I distinctly remember – that useless boy was the last one up here. Careless. Typical of kids today!'

'Oh, Sam, I don't think he . . .'

'It was him all right!' roared Old Sam. 'But at least he'll learn his lesson. His blasted pigeon's gone as well. Serve him right!'

Beryl thought better than to argue with her husband at that moment. Old Sam had been warned by the doctor not to become over-excited.

'Come on, Sam. Let's head the chickens back into the cage. Then you can have a close look at that wing. Come on, now.'

The old man's temper cooled a little as he busied himself with the task of returning the chickens to their cage. His face was still marked by heavy lines and his jaw jutted forward.

'There, Sam,' soothed Beryl. 'You catch that one and have a look at her wing and I'll pop next door and ask the neighbours. She'll turn up in someone's back garden, I expect.'

Old Sam disappeared into the cage, caught the chicken which held its wing out at an awkward angle and gently examined the feathers.

Half an hour later Beryl returned with a cup of tea for Old Sam.

'I've been to the houses on either side. No one's seen a chicken. I haven't been to the houses that back onto ours. I don't like to go where I don't know the people. Come and have your cup of tea. How's the one with the bad wing?'

Old Sam emerged from the cage and straightened. The flushed red colour had disappeared from his cheeks. Instead he looked grey and even older.

'She'll be right in a few days. Nothing broken,' he said in a cracked voice.

Beryl looked sadly at her husband.

'Would you go and ask the neighbours over the back fence? I'll see what I can do with the vegetable patch.'

Old Sam handed back the empty cup.

'Yes...' he sighed. 'But I don't think we'll find her. That crowd next door have probably got her in a cooking pot by now.'

'Sam!'

Old Sam sniffed. 'Just wait till that boy comes home.

I'll tell him, all right.'

'Sam, he's . . .' Beryl placed her hand on Old Sam's arm. 'He's only a boy. He didn't mean it.'

Old Sam walked away. 'Beryl, you're not going to stop what's got to be said. And am *I* going to tell him!'

Old Sam shuffled off to the front gate. His shoulders sagged. Beryl watched him go.

The day dragged for the old man as he waited for the boy to return. It was as if Jasper's shock would in some way make the day less painful for him.

Old Sam was standing by the chickens' cage when he heard the clink of the front gate. Jasper appeared. Old Sam got in bad moods occasionally but from the forbidding look on the old man's face Jasper instantly knew that something must be terribly wrong.

'You left the gate open.'

Jasper stopped.

'Last night. You were the last one up here. Right? And you left the blasted gate open. I came up here this morning . . . the chickens were all in the garden. Your bird's gone.'

The boy ran up to the wire of the cage and looked in disbelief.

'I've lost one of my chickens.' The low growl droned on. 'Mrs Lindsay's vegetable patch is a ruin.'

Jasper turned to face the old man. His face was strained. His eyes were moist.

Old Sam continued. 'One chicken's got a bad wing . . .'

'No . . .' Jasper choked.

Old Sam was not to be put off, '. . . and me and Mrs Lindsay have spent half the day traipsing round the neighbourhood looking for the chicken.'

34

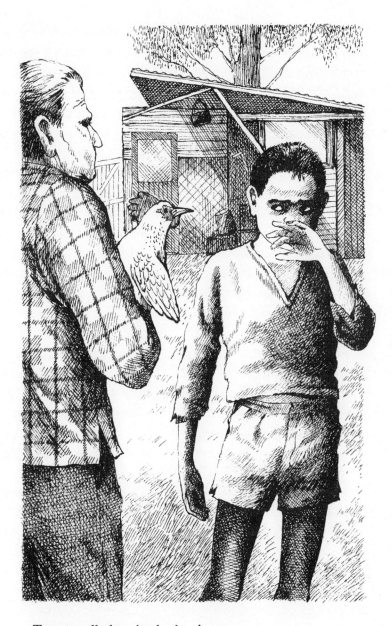

Tears welled up in the boy's eyes.
'I didn't leave the gate open, Mr Sam. I always close it

after me. I'm sure I didn't. I wouldn't want my bird to go away . . . or your chickens.'

Old Sam was not moved. 'You were the last one up here last night. No one else has been here. Had to be you.'

The boy turned to look inside the cage again, hoping everything was a mistake, hoping to see his pigeon on its perch.   Tears coursed down Jasper's brown cheeks. He wiped his nose against the back of his sleeve.

'I didn't! I didn't!' he sobbed. 'I wouldn't let my bird escape!'

Old Sam felt a lump rising in his throat but the anger he had felt earlier was still there.

'You lost a pigeon and I lost one of my chickens. Young people these days got to learn to care for things properly.'

The old man half turned and stared sadly at the ruined vegetable patch. Jasper gave a last look round the sky and roof-tops in the forlorn hope of seeing his pigeon, then ran out of Sam's garden and home where he flung himself on his bed and buried his face in the pillow.

Old Sam didn't feel any easier now that Jasper had been told. He felt worse. Had he been too hard on the boy? Not wanting to face Beryl at that moment he walked to the front garden to lean on the gate.

S·E·V·E·N

Old Sam was tired. It had been a day he wished had never happened. His head ached and his legs felt weary. He hardly noticed the rush-hour crowd at the far end of the road. But two figures noticed Old Sam in his usual place at the front gate – two boys in cricket whites on their way home after training.

'How's Esmeralda?' A pug-nosed face appeared in front of Old Sam. 'Cluck, cluck. Did Myrtle get her exercise today?' The other pug-nosed face half swallowed a laugh and hissed a curt, 'Don't!'

Old Sam instantly snapped out of his daze. His eyes narrowed. 'What did you say, boy?'

The twins sauntered off down the street. 'Bye, Mr Chickabiddy. Have a nice day!' They burst into giggles and ran off. Sam watched them until they turned past the shops at the busy highway. He rubbed the back of his hand thoughtfully against the grey stubble on his chin.

He turned at the sound of bare feet running up to him from across the picket fence. A face appeared, a young brown face with reddened eyes. Jasper couldn't speak for a moment. Fear still edged his face but so too did a strange excitement.

The boy swallowed. 'Mr Frank's back!'

Old Sam swung round. He had thought that the day's excitement was over.

Jasper continued. 'He's on the roof of the chickens' cage. He's trying to get in.'

Old Sam was unable to speak for a moment. It took a few moments for his old body to snap back into action.

''Struth! Well don't just stand there. Come over. We've got to get him in before it gets dark.'

The old man and the boy went through to the back garden and stopped by the shed.

'There he is, all right. The little beggar. Trying to get in, too.'

'I knew he would come back,' breathed the boy. 'I knew it.'

'Well, we've got to get him in safely, first, before we can start crowing, son.'

'How can we do that?' asked Jasper.

The old man opened the shed door.

'You walk up to the cage door – very slowly, like – open the door wide, then move slowly back.'

'What about the chickens?'

'They won't get far with us standing here. You go on. Gently now. No sudden movements.'

Jasper, head down, hardly daring to look up at the pigeon, crept towards the cage. For a moment he thought the pigeon might fly off but it only scrabbled over the wire roof to the far end. The boy carefully opened the door, then stepped back. The chickens looked at him strangely but didn't move towards the open door. Old Sam edged up, gently calling the names of his chickens as he threw them some wheat. He aimed some at the pigeon's platform too, then joined Jasper at the shed.

They watched, not daring to talk. The bird seemed hungry and eager to join the chickens in their unexpected meal. It bobbed its head through the chicken wire.

'The door, the door . . . ' breathed Jasper.

'There he goes, son,' said Old Sam with a sigh of relief as the bird suddenly flew in a tight arc straight through the door and onto his platform. 'Home!' smiled Old Sam. 'Go and close the door, son.'

Jasper walked quickly to the door, closed it and fastened the latch. He couldn't take his eyes off the bird. Old Sam came up behind Jasper and the pair watched in silence. Mr Frank seemed pleased to be home. His crop looked empty and his beak darted eagerly at every grain of wheat on the platform. The bird flew down to the drinking trough and took two long draughts of water, holding its head high as it swallowed. Then it returned to its platform, ruffled its feathers and settled for the night, unconcerned at the grinning faces the other side of the wire.

'Well, it's been a day,' sighed Old Sam as they turned to leave.

Jasper stopped and looked up at Old Sam.

'I, I'm sure I didn't leave the door open. I had a think about it. I'm sure I didn't.'

Old Sam looked embarrassed. His voice was a throaty rumble.

'I had a think, too. I believe you. You go home now. We'll talk about it tomorrow.' Jasper turned towards the front gate. 'Son . . . I'm glad your Mr Frank returned.' Jasper looked down at his feet. 'Tell me, how did you know he had come back?'

Jasper looked up. 'I heard wings. I think I did, anyway.'

Old Sam smiled. 'Off you go. I'll see you tomorrow. I'll tell Mrs Lindsay the good news. Lord knows she could do with some.'

E·I·G·H·T

The next day was Saturday. Old Sam had hurried off to the shops without telling Beryl why he was going. After lunch he waited for Jasper at the chickens' cage. The boy wondered if the old man would still be angry.

'Come on, boy, come on!' enthused Old Sam when he saw Jasper approaching slowly. 'What do you think?' Old Sam was in an unusually good mood.

Jasper looked but couldn't notice anything different. Frank was perched on his platform looking very much at home. Jasper's eyes settled on Old Sam's box of tools and some pieces of wood near the cage door.

'The tools?'

'No,' laughed Old Sam. 'Look . . . here!' The old man walked up to the cage door and rattled a shiny new padlock. 'I bought it today. What do you think?'

Jasper wasn't sure what to say. 'It's good.'

'Course it's good! It'll stop anyone getting at our birds. Look, it came with two keys. One for me,' said Old Sam as his fingers worked at the key ring, 'and one for you. There.'

The boy took the key. Surprise showed on his face.

'What do you say?' The old man had been waiting impatiently for the boy to visit so that he could give him the key.

Jasper took the key. 'Thank you.' He looked up at the old man's face. 'I'll keep it in a secret place in my bedroom.'

Old Sam laughed. 'Kids! Anyway, this is what we're up to today.' He sorted through his tool-box and stood up holding a pencil. 'Right here,' said Sam as he drew a small square on the wooden wall of the cage. 'We're going to build a trap.'

'A trap?' Jasper's forehead wrinkled.

'Yep. It's like a personal little doorway for your Mr Frank. High enough so that cats can't get in. Small enough so that my old chickens won't be interested. And some wires hanging down so that he can get in, but he can't get out. He only gets out when we let him. Hand me the chisel. And the hammer.'

Old Sam busied himself with the trap. Jasper helped. First the old man cut a pigeon-sized square into the wall. Then he nailed a small landing platform to the outside. The wires were more difficult. He first bent some fencing wire into three sets of wire loops. Then he stapled the loops inside the cage above the square hole so that they could move freely inwards, but were stopped from swinging outwards by the wall.

'There,' puffed Sam. 'Doesn't take long with two doing it. This is how it works. We let Mr Frank out for a fly around – preferably when he's hungry. That's so he'll want to come back. Then, he lands on this platform, pushes his head through the wire like this . . . ' Old Sam pushed his hand through the wire loops, ' . . . and flies back inside. Simple. And he can't fly out because those wires don't bend back the other way. See?'

Jasper was unsure. 'How will Mr Frank know he's supposed to do that?' asked Jasper.

Old Sam roared with laughter. 'Ha! He'll know all right because we'll teach him. Give him some lessons!'

'Lessons?'

'Yep. Right now. Go in and catch him. Carefully, like I showed you. Walk up to him, wait until he's steady, then shoot your two hands round him so that his wings are pressed to his sides. Try not to let him flap about and panic himself.' Jasper caught the bird and met Old Sam outside the cage. 'All right, Mr Frank. Lesson one. How to return to your cage. Let me have him.'

Jasper handed the bird to the old man. Old Sam walked

round the back of the garden holding the pigeon so that it could see what was happening. He walked up to the trap, placed the pigeon gently through the wire loops and let it fly back to its perch.

'There!' said Old Sam. 'Now, you go in and catch him again and do what I did. About four or five times.' He noticed the boy's puzzled face. 'It's getting him used to the trap. So he knows where it is from the outside, like, and how to get in. Go on, now.'

Old Sam rested on his bench and watched Jasper.

'Right. That's enough,' puffed Old Sam as he got to his feet. You've got a nice way of handling that pigeon. A real natural.'

Jasper smiled.

'Now, go and get a handful of wheat. I'll catch the bird.' Jasper brought the wheat back to the cage. 'Let him see it. That's right. And put a few grains on the platform of the trap. Here, take the bird.'

Jasper took hold of the bird and looked up at Old Sam.

'Now, throw him up into the air.'

'What?' asked Jasper, alarmed.

'Go on.' Jasper looked doubtful, but after a close look at the bird he threw it into the air. The pigeon flapped its wings and rose high into the air. It circled the cage. The strong wings beat effortlessly. Jasper watched, entranced.

'Come on. Stand over here out of the way so he can come back.' Jasper and Old Sam stood by the shed. After a few more circles the pigeon flew straight to the platform, landed, and pecked at the few grains of wheat. Then, after one unsuccessful attempt, it pushed through the hanging wires and flew to its platform.

Jasper raced up to the cage. Old Sam followed. The boy's eyes were wide.

'He's a real good flyer. Real good!'

Old Sam stood behind Jasper. They watched the bird pecking at the wheat.

'A thoroughbred, all right. A real good bird, like you said. It's a good sign he didn't land on a roof but came straight back in.'

Jasper smiled.

'Yes, a *real* good bird. I've got an idea,' said Sam. 'Come and see me tomorrow. Early!'

N·I·N·E

'A clean shirt and a pair of shoes,' beamed Old Sam. 'And you make sure you really do ask your mother's permission. We're going for a ride in the country. A train ride. And Mr Frank's coming, too.'

Jasper ran home, still not quite sure what Old Sam had in mind but pleased to be going on a trip. Ten minutes later he presented himself at Old Sam's back door. A warm sun filled the Sunday morning stillness. A perfect day. Mrs Lindsay smiled at the boy. His hair had been brushed and he wore a clean white shirt which was almost the right size, though the sleeves were rolled up to his elbows. He was even wearing his best sand-shoes.

'Sam wants you to catch your pigeon and bring him down here. He's still getting himself ready. He said to get a hurry on.'

When Jasper reappeared holding the bird in his hands, Mrs Lindsay ushered him in.

'Sam? The boy's here.'

Old Sam appeared. He was wearing a double-breasted

blue suit which looked as if it had been hanging in a wardrobe for years.

'Couldn't find my black shoes, Beryl,' said Old Sam as he came bustling in. 'Ah, you've got the bird. Good boy. Bring him in here.'

They went into the kitchen and Sam opened the lid of a cane basket.

'In here. I've lined the bottom with newspaper. It's all right.'

Jasper was doubtful, but he put the bird into the cane basket and the old man fastened the lid.

'I know what you're thinking – but it's all right. There's air holes round the back. See?'

Old Sam grunted as he bent down to put on the shoes which Beryl had brought.

'Right! Mrs Lindsay's packed us a picnic hamper for lunch. And a thermos of tea. Come on. We've got a train to catch. You asked your mother, didn't you?'

At the last moment Old Sam couldn't find his Sunday hat. They were running late when they walked through the front gate. Beryl waved them off. Jasper carried the basket with the pigeon and Old Sam carried the picnic hamper.

It was only a short walk to the station. Old Sam paid for the tickets and they walked across the foot-bridge to the platform. There were only two other people waiting for the train.

'Mustn't forget to change at Central,' panted Old Sam. Then the train came.

The train journey seemed to take ages. The other passengers looked suspiciously at the cane basket every time Mr Frank shuffled or made a noise. Jasper was embarrassed and pretended not to notice.

At last Old Sam stood up. 'This is our stop.'

Jasper was surprised to see houses and shops when he had expected farms or forest. Old Sam sensed the boy's feelings.

'This is far enough for Mr Frank's first long flight. I was sent here to do my training during the war. It was mostly bush around here then. Now that *was* donkey's years ago. Turn left here and we should find the parade ground.. That is, if they haven't built hamburger bars or houses all over it.'

They entered a large, flat grassed area. Very few people were about. In the distance two boys were unsuccessfully trying to fly a kite.

'Now, we'll let your bird go. But I must tell you, son, there's a risk – a small risk. He could get taken by a hawk or he might decide he doesn't like our place. But I've got a feeling he'll be home before us. I reckon he's a champion. A thoroughbred. What do you say?'

Jasper looked at the sky and then at the old man's face.

'Could he really be home before us? All that way?' he asked, amazed.

'Why,' laughed Old Sam, 'I'd even bet a week's pension on it. But don't you tell Mrs Lindsay I said that!' Old Sam laughed so hard he started coughing. 'It's up to you, son.'

Jasper knelt down with his head close to the basket.

'You make sure you go straight home, now, Mr Frank. I hope you know the way.' He looked up at Old Sam who gave a reassuring nod of his head. Instantly the bird struggled to the top of the basket and flapped into the air.

Old Sam and Jasper, shielding their eyes from the sun, watched the bird circle twice and head off into the distance. They watched, not speaking, until the pigeon was a speck in the cloudless sky.

When it had disappeared from sight Jasper said, 'Is he going the right way?'

'I reckon so,' answered Old Sam. 'Don't you go worrying. I don't know how they do it. Pigeons, I mean. Hundreds of miles. Finding their way. Don't reckon the scientists know for sure, either. Let's go and have our lunch under that tree over there.'

As they ate their sandwiches Old Sam talked of the times he had marched over the parade ground, of rows of tents and camp fires and of the fine men he had known. Jasper half listened but his mind was really on the pigeon. Would a hawk notice his bird? Would it find its way home? How did Mr Frank know the way? He kept thinking of the small, frail shape disappearing into the wide horizon. Would he ever see Mr Frank again?

As they boarded the train to return home Old Sam said, 'I reckon your Frank's home now and having himself a fine feed of pigeon peas. I asked Mrs Lindsay to put some in the cage for him after we'd gone. Heh!'

Jasper smiled. Old Sam dozed on the train and if it wasn't for Jasper they would have missed the change at Central station.

Walking home from the station Jasper noticed that Old Sam was limping. He slowed his pace to keep with the old man, but he couldn't wait to get home and check on his pigeon. As they turned into Albert Road they stopped abruptly. The man from the newsagency on the corner was standing with his arms folded, glaring. An angry man was shouting at two boys, identical, with pug-noses and short, bristly hair. The angry man pointed up to a broken window. The two boys were trying to look angelic.

' . . . no pocket money, because you're *both* going to pay for it. And no cricket training! Banned! And if you two don't smarten up your ideas . . . '

Jasper and Old Sam looked at each other. A faint trace of a smile flickered at the corners of the old man's tired face. They walked on.

Beryl met them at the front gate. 'He beat you!' she

laughed. 'He came home ages ago. What kept you two slow coaches?'

'The pigeon didn't have to change trains!' laughed Old Sam.

Jasper's face was alive. 'Are you coming up to see Mr Frank?' asked the boy.

'You go up, son. I'll go inside and rest up. I told you he was a champion, didn't I?'

'He sure is a champion,' said Jasper. 'A thoroughbred.'

Old Sam gave a laugh, but Beryl looked concerned.

'Are you all right, Sam?' she asked.

'Don't you go fussing,' Old Sam replied grumpily. 'Off you go now, son. Come and tell me about your Frank before you go home.'

At the cage Jasper stopped. Even though Mrs Lindsay had told them the bird was safely home the boy still gazed in amazement.

With face pressed to the wire, his eyes looked up at the bird. The last time he had seen Mr Frank the bird was a small speck in the sky. The pigeon sat on his high perch and settled, ready for the night, unaware of the small boy gazing up in admiration.

T·E·N

At school the next day Jasper could only think of his pigeon and the way it had flown back to the cage and beaten them home. At last, when school was over for the day, Jasper ran all the way to Old Sam's back garden. The old man wasn't up at the cage so the boy knocked on the back door. Mrs Lindsay appeared.

'Hello,' said Jasper, still with a touch of shyness. 'Is Mr Sam coming up to feed the chickens?'

Mrs Lindsay looked at the boy for a moment. Her usually cheerful face looked sad.

'Sam's not well today, son. He asked if you wouldn't mind seeing to them today. You've got your own key, haven't you?'

'Sure,' said Jasper. 'I'll do it.'

The boy ran to the shed and filled a scoop with wheat. He stopped outside the cage and looked in. Mr Frank was acting strangely. Jasper stood and watched for ten minutes then ran back to Old Sam's door.

'Finished already?' asked Mrs Lindsay as she opened the door.

'No,' replied Jasper. 'It's Mr Frank. He's doing something different. Could Mr Sam come up and see?'

Mrs Lindsay thought for a moment. 'I don't rightly know, son. Wait here a minute. I'll go and ask Sam.'

Five minutes later Old Sam appeared. He was wrapped in an old blue checked dressing gown, had slippers on his feet and leaned on a walking stick. The white stubble on his chin showed that he hadn't shaved.

'Hello, young feller.' His voice croaked. 'What's the matter?'

Jasper explained.

'Reckon I'd better come up and have a look,' said the old man. With slow steps Old Sam walked to the cage. The old man and the boy looked in at the pigeon. Mr Frank was flying down to the bottom of the cage and picking up pieces of grass, then flying up to the wooden box and dropping the pieces in.

'Well I'll be!' sighed Old Sam, then gave a chuckle.

'Why is he doing that?' asked Jasper, looking up at the old man.

'If I'm not mistaken, your Frank is building a nest! You know what that means?'

Jasper shook his head.

'It means that your Frank must be a hen bird – a *lady*. What do you think of that?'

'Mr Frank?' asked Jasper. 'A lady?'

'Yep.' Old Sam looked thoughtful and rubbed the back of his hand on his stubbly chin. 'If the bird's making a nest it can only mean one thing – she'll be laying some eggs soon. But if the eggs are fertile, you know, if they hatch – she must have mated when she was out of the cage.

Probably that day when the chickens got out. Well I'll be!'

They stared at the bird.

'You know,' said Old Sam, 'I was thinking the other day that I might get a mate for your bird. So that it wasn't lonely. But with eggs on the way . . . I tell you what, if she has young ones she'll be busy looking after them herself. You'll need to keep a close eye on her.'

Jasper still couldn't believe it.

'Mr Frank – is a lady!'

Old Sam laughed. 'Well, you've got a problem now. You'll have to give it a different name. You can't call a hen bird Mr Frank!'

Jasper thought for a moment. 'No problem. I'll call her Mrs Frank.'

'Mrs Frank!' exclaimed Old Sam. 'Well I'll be. Kids these days!' The old man's laughter turned to a coughing fit.

When he had recovered Old Sam placed a hand on Jasper's shoulder. When he spoke his voice had a strange, wheezy sound.

'Son, there's something I've got to tell you. I've got to go into hospital for a few days. They tell me it's nothing serious, but Mrs Lindsay . . . she worries. You know what she's like. I was wondering if you could do a favour for me.'

The boy suddenly felt cold. His voice sounded small. 'Sure . . . Anything.'

'I was wondering if you'd mind looking after my chickens while I'm away. I know I can trust you to look after them. And, if you wouldn't mind . . . to pop in to say hello to Mrs Lindsay. She'd like that.' His voice trailed off. Jasper nodded his head. The old man brightened. 'Let's go back down, now. We'll tell Mrs Lindsay the news about *Mrs* Frank. She'll be tickled pink.'

The two friends headed for the kitchen.